MIMI

takes charge

By Agnès Rosenstiehl

**Published in the United States of America
by Advocacy Press
P.O. Box 236
Santa Barbara, CA 93102, USA**

Text Copyright © Advocacy Press, 1991

All other rights © Bayard Presse, 1987

First published in France as "Mimi Cracra" under the imprint
POMME D'API-CENTURION JEUNESSE

 Advocacy Press is a division of Advocates for Girls, a non-profit corporation in
support of Girls Incorporated of Greater Santa Barbara and Girls Incorporated.

Edited by Sandy Stryker and Penelope C. Paine

Layout design: Barbara Boros
Text handwritten by: Janice Blair

Library of Congress Cataloging-in-Publication Data

ISBN 0-911655-50-6

Printed in Singapore

**Special thanks to: Kyle Jean Brace, Allana Elvoson, Ph.D., Judith Harber, The Kiers Family, Itoko Maeno,
Nancy Rose, Madeleine Roston, William P. Sheehan, Alan M. Smith and Jean Whigham**

Hello,

   Have you ever made a mask from a pancake, or dressed up like a zebra? My name's Mimi, and I do exciting things like this every day. Though I'm quite small, I love to see and explore all the wonders I've found in my world. I have two special friends, my teddy bear, Coco, and my doll, Cecelia. My best friend, though, is my imagination. I use it to make up games, and to find different uses for things like my hat, my pencils, and my boots. Once I made a typewriter out of empty egg cartons. You can read about more of my adventures in this book. Come along won't you? And bring your imagination!

Your Friend,
Mimi

Mimi Plays Doctor

A good doctor is always there when you need her.

What's happened to your finger, Coco? Were you stung by a bee?

This soothing cream of spider spit will make it stop stinging!

Oh, Cecelia, I bet you have a headache! And does everything look upside-down?

I'm going to be a dynamite doctor
when I grow up.
What do you want to do when you are older?

Mimi Samples the Candy

Candy is one of my favorite things.
What are some of yours?

Mimi Smells a Daisy

14

Or as strong! There are so many good smells.
Can you name some?

Mimi Plays in the Dark

I like to play in the dark.

It's like having my eyes closed, except I can do so many more things.

Especially if I have my flashlight.

I hope it stays dark for a long time.
Do you like the dark ?

Mimi Eats a Pancake

21

What should I make next? I bet
green cupcakes would be great for ear muffs!
Do you like to make things?

Mimi Dresses Up

I like being me, but sometimes it's interesting to be someone else.

This striped shirt looks like something a zebra would wear!

But it doesn't quite match my face.

These paints should do the trick.

Maybe I'll sleep in the grass tonight as zebras do!
Can you think of some other animals
which sleep in the grass?

Mimi Feeds Coco

Babies need a lot of love and care.
Have you ever helped to feed a real baby?

Mimi Makes a Birthday Cake

Whenever I see a cake, I think about parties.

This cake would be perfect for Coco's birthday.

I'll need some pencils to use as pretend candles.

Don't look, Coco! It's a surprise!

33

I wonder when it will be my birthday?
When will it be yours?
How many candles will you have on your cake?

Mimi Feeds the Trash Can

Feeding the trash can is an important job!
Remember to feed yours, too! They love garbage.

Mimi Shovels Sand

It takes a long time to finish big jobs!
Does someone in your family work all day long?

Mimi's

**Here are some more things
I enjoy doing. Maybe you will, too!**

🦋 Find new ways to enjoy healthy things: like brushing your teeth (sometimes I pretend my mouth is a washing machine), washing your hands (soap is a <u>great</u> invention), taking a walk (so much to see), drinking a glass of water (I like to feel it run down into my tummy), or singing a song (I have a wonderful voice. I bet you do too).

🦋 Notice the tastes and smells of different foods, as well as the way other things around you smell (plants, pets, the air after it rains, clean clothes, clean hair, for example). Maybe a grownup will let you smell and taste things like lemon, salt, or cinnamon. What things smell bad? What things smell dangerous? What is your favorite taste and smell?

🦋 Night is a time of rest even for the sun and many plants and animals. Many people say you should count sheep to help you get to sleep. But I prefer to think about all the exciting things I will do and learn in the morning.

🦋 Play with cars, blocks, and mud as well as dolls and makeup!

🦋 Use your imagination to see new things in, or find new uses for, the things around you. Can you see pictures in the clouds? Find a forest in your salad or make a house under the kitchen table!

🦋 Collect old clothes and shoes, and keep them in a dress-up box. Old makeup is great, too, if it comes off with soap and water. Sometimes I like to dress up like people I see around me. But I also collect pictures of people in other parts of the world. It's fun to pretend I'm them, too!

🦋 Help take care of a baby (well, at least, someone younger than you), or a pet like a cat, dog, parrot, or even a snail! Find out what they like to eat, and how you can help them feel safe and loved.

Bright Ideas!

🌸 Make birthday parties for your friends, pets, dolls, and stuffed animals. That way, you can make many more birthday wishes!

🌸 Ask if you can help sort the trash for recycling, or help carry it out. If you have a garden, you can even feed the soil with peels and skins!

🌸 Taking care of a home and family is a big job, so I try to help as much as I can. Maybe, like me, you can clear off the kitchen counter or bring in the mail every day. Washing the dog can be fun, too. It takes a lot of energy!

🌸 Grownups do many jobs when they're away from home. Ask the ones you know what they do at work all day. Notice, too, what jobs people are doing when you go shopping or to the bank or post office or doctor's office. Draw pictures of some of these people working. Which kinds of work look most interesting to you?

🌸 Memorize your address and telephone number. Knowing them will help you be safe.

🌸 Think of as many uses as you can for a paper grocery bag.

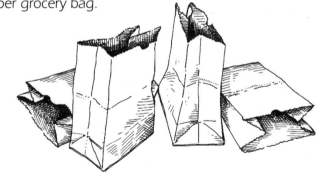

For a list of ideas, write to me at
   Advocacy Press,
   P.O. Box 236
   Santa Barbara, CA 93102

Enjoy and learn! Happy playing!

A NOTE ON GROWNUPS: There are more of them around than you might think! Moms, dads, big sisters and brothers, aunts, uncles, grandparents, godparents, family friends, neighbors, babysitters, and child care providers all make good grownups. Don't overlook them! Learn from them what you can!

Color and Write Your Own Story

Other books by Advocacy Press

Positive rhymes for all children:

Mother Nature Nursery Rhymes, by Mother Nature. Illustrated by Itoko Maeno. 9"x12". Hardcover with dustjacket, 32 pages, full-color illustrations throughout. ISBN 0-911655-01-8 $14.95

Father Gander Nursery Rhymes, by Father Gander. Illustrated by Carolyn Blattel. 9"x12". Hardcover with dustjacket, 48 pages, full-color illustrations throughout. ISBN 0-911655-12-3 $14.95

Help build self-esteem with Minou, Kylie, Tonia, Sally and Horatio:

Minou, by Mindy Bingham. Illustrated by Itoko Maeno. 9"x12". Hardcover with dustjacket, 64 pages, full-color illustrations throughout. ISBN 0-911655-36-0 $14.95

My Way Sally, by Mindy Bingham and Penelope C. Paine. Illustrated by Itoko Maeno. 9"x12". Hardcover with dustjacket, 48 pages, full-color illustrations throughout. ISBN 0-911655-27-1 $14.95

Kylie's Song, by Patty Sheehan. Illustrated by Itoko Maeno. 9"x12". Hardcover with dustjacket, 32 pages, full-color illustrations throughout. ISBN 0--911655-19-0 $13.95

Tonia the Tree, by Sandy Stryker. Illustrated by Itoko Maeno. 9"x12". Hardcover with dustjacket, 32 pages, full-color illustrations throughout. ISBN 0-911655-16-6 $13.95

Time for Horatio, by Penelope C. Paine. Illustrated by Itoko Maeno. 9"x12". Hardcover with dustjacket, 48 pages, full-color illustrations throughout. ISBN 0-911655-33-6 $14.95

Also available: *Berta Benz and the Motorwagen*, by Mindy Bingham. Illustrated by Itoko Maeno. 9"x12". Hardcover with dustjacket, 48 pages, full-color illustrations throughout. ISBN 0-911655-38-7 $14.95

Other books in the MIMI series:

1. *Mimi Takes Charge* ISBN 0-911655-50-6

2. *Mimi Makes A Splash* ISBN 0-911655-51-4

3. *Mimi Moves Ahead*, publication date: November 1991

4. *Mimi Makes a Mark*, publication date: November 1991

5. *Mimi Takes the Stage*, publication date: June 1992

6. *Mimi Finds Friends*, publication date: June 1992

7. *Mimi Shows the Way*, publication date: June 1992

Each graphic picture book contains ten stories and activity pages. 8" x 91/4" Softcover, 48 pages. $6.95 Hardcover, $14.95

You can find Advocacy Press books at better bookstores. Or you may order them directly by sending a check for the total amount due plus $2.50 for shipping and handling per book to: Advocacy Press, P.O. Box 236, Dept. A, Santa Barbara, California 93102-0236. For your review, we will be happy to send you more information on these publications.